PECK PECK PECK

Lucy Cousins

WALKER BOOKS
AND SUBSIDIARIES
LONDON · BOSTON · SYDNEY · AUCKLAND

Today my daddy
said to me,

"It's time you learnt
to peck a tree."

"Now hold on tight,
that's very good.
Then peck,
peck,
peck,
peck,
peck the wood."

PECK PECK PECK

"Oh look, yippee!

I've pecked a hole
right through this tree."

"Darling, you're such
a CLEVER BIRD.
That hole you've pecked
is SO SUPERB.

Now off you go,
my little one.
Practise hard
and have some fun."

So off I flew,
I couldn't wait,
across the grass,
onto the gate.

And now I'll peck
this big blue door,
then go inside
and peck some more.

PECK
PECK
PECK

I peck the hat,
I peck the mat,
   the tennis racket
and the jacket.

PECK PECK PECK

a magazine,
a picture of
Aunt Geraldine,

an armchair,
a teddy bear
and a book
Called Jane Eyre.

I
peck
the
shirt,

I
peck
the
skirt,

I
peck
the
slippers

and the knickers.

PECK

PECK

PECK

PECK

PECK

I peck the soap,

the blue shampoo,

I peck the sink,

I peck the loo.

PECK PECK PECK

a tangerine,
a nectarine,
● a green bean,
an aubergine,
a sardine, ●
some margarine ●

●

and seventeen jelly beans.

I peck and peck and peck and peck.

I peck,
peck,
peck,
peck,
peck,
peck,
peck,
until there's NOTHING LEFT to peck.

I've pecked and pecked,

I've been so busy,

but now I'm tired

and rather dizzy.

I think

I'll fly back to my nest,
find my dad
and have a rest.

"Oh Daddy, I've had
so much fun.
You should see
the holes I've done.

I absolutely
LOVE to peck.
I love, love, love,
love, LOVE to peck."

"That's fantastic,"
Daddy said.
"And now it's time
you went to bed.

Goodnight, sleep tight,
I love you.
I love, love, love,
love, LOVE you."